The Pirates on Holiday

By Adam and Charlotte Guillain

Illustrated by Rupert Van Wyk

FRANKLIN WATTS

LONDON • SYDNEY

Chapter 1

Business was booming for the Planktown Pirates. Their treasure chests were bulging with the gold coins they had found.

All the crew had splashed out and bought themselves new hats.

But the Planktown Pirates were tired after working so hard.

"We need a break," groaned Captain Cuttlefish.

"A holiday!" sighed Connor the Cabin Boy. "But I've seen enough tropical islands and palm trees to last me a lifetime," grumbled Manta Ray Jack, the ship's first mate.

As the pirates scratched their heads and wondered what to do, the postman rowed up. "Pirate post!" he shouted as he threw a pile of letters onto the deck. Cook Cockles picked up the post and held up a brochure.

"Windy View Caravan Park," he read.

"The most fun you'll ever have on holiday."

"That's it," cried Captain Cuttlefish.

"Pack your bags, boys! I've always wanted

to go to a holiday camp. Anchors away!

We're setting sail for Windy View!"

Chapter 2

By teatime, the pirates had left the warm blue waters of Planktown far behind, and were lowering their anchor in Windy View harbour. The sky was a dark grey and a bitterly cold wind howled onto shore.

The pirates shivered as they carried their bags up to the campsite.

"Welcome to Windy View! I'm Dennis," smiled the man at the desk. He glanced at Cook Cockles' cooking knives.

"You won't need those," he said. "You're on holiday now! All your meals will be cooked for you at the canteen."

"Here's your caravan," said Dennis.

"It looks, er, very cosy," said Manta Ray Jack.

"There's a sea view," said Dennis, and he proudly pointed between the other caravans.

The pirates looked at one another.

"It's lovely," said Captain Cuttlefish.

"Let's get unpacked."

Chapter 3

The pirates soon unpacked and settled in.

It was a bit of a squash in the caravan so

they went to the canteen for dinner.

The lady behind the counter looked at

them suspiciously.

"We've only got fish, chips and mushy peas,"
she snapped. "And jam roly-poly for pudding."

"Thank you," said Captain Cuttlefish.

"Get in line, crew."

The lady slopped food onto each pirate's
plate and they found a table to sit together.

"Dig in me hearties," said the Captain.

The fish was cold. The chips were soggy.

The peas were slushy.

"I miss Cook Cockles' pies," moaned

Manta Ray Jack.

"Maybe pudding will be better," said
Connor hopefully. It wasn't.

"I can't find any jam," muttered
Cook Cockles. Captain Cuttlefish sighed.

"Let's go to bed," Captain Cuttlefish said.

"We'll start our holiday tomorrow."

So the pirates trailed back to their caravan

and squeezed into

their bunks.

"Goodnight crew," said Captain Cuttlefish,

switching off the light.

"Goodnight Captain," they replied.

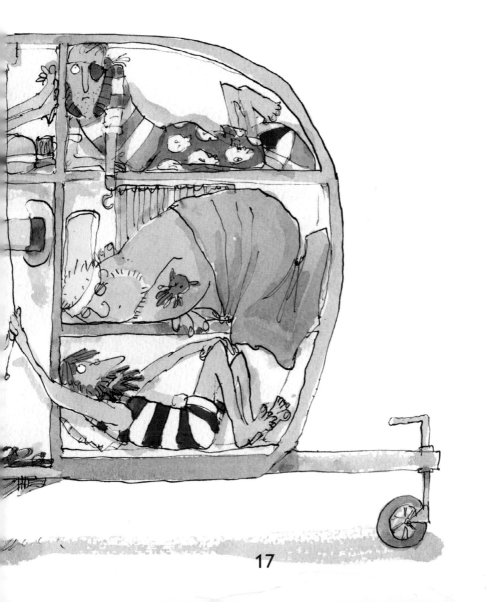

Chapter 4

Next morning, the pirates rolled out of bed groaning and rubbing their eyes.

"I didn't sleep all night," mumbled Connor.

"Neither did I," sighed Captain Cuttlefish. "Not a wink! I missed the ocean rocking me to sleep."

After breakfast, the pirates went out to explore. There was plenty to do and they were keen to join in.

Manta Ray Jack loved the disco, but he was asked to leave when his dance moves got dangerous.

The swimming pool looked like fun but the pirates weren't allowed to row their boat in it.

Then they got told off for using the diving board as a plank and making the other holidaymakers walk off it.

"What can we do?" wailed Cook Cockles.

Just then Captain Cuttlefish saw a poster.

"Pirate party! Come dressed as a pirate. Prizes for the best costume and pirate songs."

"It's this afternoon!" he cried. "Come on crew! Let's go and win some prizes!"

Chapter Five

The pirates felt at home when they got to the party. There were peg legs and parrots. There were jolly rogers and treasure chests.

"Line up for the pirate costume competition!" shouted Dennis, who was wearing an eyepatch.

Captain Cuttlefish eagerly joined the line of children in their fancy dress and winked at his crew.

The judges walked up and down the line and whispered to each other before making their decision.

"And the winner is... Jimmy!"

declared Dennis.

Captain Cuttlefish stared

in disbelief.

"Curses and barnacles – that's not fair!

His costume's rubbish!" he shouted.

Dennis glared at the Captain.

"Time for pirate songs," Dennis announced.

The Planktown Pirates sang their hearts out.

They were sure that they would be the best.

"And the winners are... Daisy and Polly,

who also played the recorder beautifully,"

said Dennis.

"NO!" shouted the crew.

"That wasn't a proper pirate song!"

yelled Manta Ray Jack.

"And pirates don't play recorders!"

bellowed Cook Cockles.

Dennis pointed to the door.

"Come on crew," said Captain Cuttlefish. "I've had enough of this holiday. Let's get back to our ship and go back to work."

The Planktown Pirates cheered as they raced down the harbour. Who needed a holiday when being a pirate was the best job in the world?

First published in 2013 by
Franklin Watts
338 Euston Road
London
NW1 3BH

Franklin Watts Australia
Level 17/207 Kent Street
Sydney
NSW 2000

Text © Adam and Charlotte Guillain 2013
Illustration © Rupert Van Wyk 2013

The rights of Adam and Charlotte Guillain to
be identified as the authors and Rupert Van
Wyk as the illustrator of this Work have been
asserted in accordance with the Copyright,
Designs and Patents Act, 1988.

Series Editor: Melanie Palmer
Editor: Jackie Hamley
Series Advisor: Catherine Glavina
Series Designer: Peter Scoulding

A CIP catalogue record for this book is
available from the British Library.

ISBN 978 1 4451 2644 9 (hbk)
ISBN 978 1 4451 2650 0 (pbk)
ISBN 978 1 4451 2662 3 (library ebook)

Printed in China

Franklin Watts is a division of Hachette
Children's Books, an Hachette UK company.
www.hachette.co.uk